THE LAST

BY

COLIN NORMAN

This novel is entirely a work of fiction. The names, characters and incidents portrayed in it are the work of the author's imagination. Any resemblance to actual persons, living or dead, events or localities is entirely coincidental.

All rights reserved. No part of this publication may be reproduced, stored in a retrieval system, or transmitted, in any form or by any means, electronic, mechanical, photocopying, recording or otherwise, except as permitted by the UK copyright, Designs and Patents Act 1988, without the prior permission of the publisher.

Dedicated

to my

friends and family

Other Books by the Author.

Fiction:

The Man Who Never Was

A Near Miss From The Past

The Golden Adversity

An Unforgettable Memory

The Last Chance

NON Fiction:

Reach For The Stars: A story of transferring Social housing to a Housing Association

A Lifetimes Achievement: My journey and story of over 47 years

SYNOPSIS

THE LAST CHANCE

Bret has sold his holdings in his business of rental housing, to a bigger company.
He decided to have a short break to the east coast before he planned the next part of his future.
When in a café, he met an old friend from the forces with land he wanted to develop, that Bret was interested in.
The adventure begins when Russians, who owned the adjoining land, put pressure on him. Bret contacted a friend and was told of the MI5 interest. Bret gets more involved when his friend Mike, who works for MI5, contacts him and Bret is invited for dinner by the Russians who want the land.
Things all change when Bret's friend Arthur is in a plane crash, leaving his business and all his holdings to Bret.
What follows is Bret being kidnapped and then getting more involved with MI5.
With many unexpected turns, this adventure finishes with a final twist.

THE LAST CHANCE.

CHAPTER 1

It all begins.

The spring and the sunshine had arrived late this year and I had nearly given up going away for a break. Although I knew, I needed one after a very hard few months of negotiations and arranging my company of rented accommodation becoming, what they term as a public company.

I have done this to allow my tenants the chances of being a part of a well-run larger housing group. Who could provide the management and new accommodation my tenants and their children, could now transfer to for larger homes. Plus, they and their grown up, children can if they wish, have a choice of renting or shared ownership. Plus, the upkeep of all the properties would be maintained in top class condition.
It had been a hard, but fair agreement to allow my take over. Now, at last, I had the money from the sale of my company and a position on their board to still have a say in the direction of the group's

future and any further expansion they plan for.

I had decided I would go to the east coast for a break and at the moment, I'm in my car driving to my favoured area. I have been on the road 2 hours but, it still would take another hour to drive to the hotel, I had decided on.

As I noticed a café coming up, I turned into its car park and parked. Got out and walked to the entrance door. It was not busy inside and I chose a table put my bag down on the chair and went to the counter, ordered tea and toast then sat down at my table I had chosen, which was facing the car parking area.

I sat relaxing, looking out at the car parking area, when I suddenly noticed a car stop and a male got out, who had a very familiar face. I watched him and the lady he was with walk towards the café entrance and come in.
Now he was closer I knew it was who I thought it was and as he walked talking to the lady by my table I stood up and said to him smiling, "In all the cafes in all the world, I bump into you!"

He stopped and turned to look at me. His face broke into a big smile and replied, "You old reprobate I thought you was dead!" We shook hands and he introduced me to his girl beside him.

"This is Bret Mann a friend and colleague from my years in the forces, who I thought was dead, having left the regiment before I did and neither of us communicating for many years. Bret may I introduce a colleague of mine Lucy Wells my PA."

I shook hands with her and invited them to join me at my table.

His name is Arthur Lee who after leaving the forces joined his family business in the construction of houses, flats, etc and over the years had expanded to a profitable well-run company, which he was now chair of. This I know from my contacts in the rental trade.

He was soon explaining to me he had a small estate in Norfolk in the area near to Cromer, with his own small cabin in the woods. He was also looking to develop some of it into a chalet and touring Caravan Park as it goes down to the sea with a private beach.

I remarked now how I was a man of leisure and was looking around to invest in property and I may be interested in his development area to invest in.

He seemed delighted and asked if I had time to

follow him now to the estate and he would show me his plans and take me round the area to look at the possibility of developing it.

We finished our snack and set off with him leading the way to his estate.

It only took 40 minutes to get there, and we drove up the road to the cabin and parked.

Arthur opened the door we all entered it, Arthur leading. He asked if I had time now to view the area which he intended to develop.
I agreed to, and Lucy asked to accompany us. We agreed and within 10 minutes we were on the way to the area in his car.

It was an area on the edge of the woods that had a potential for brick-built chalets and an area of field near to the trees on the top of the cliff for a touring caravan site, I judged.

In fact, seeing it made me excited to get it surveyed and plans to be drawn up by a firm I knew well and would do the survey also.

I also agreed to be a partner with Arthur financially, in an equal partnership, which he eagerly jumped at. So on return to the cabin, we shook hands and I arranged to see him in a week's time to be agreed by our PAs. Before I left, we agreed to meet the next evening for a meal at a place he was known at.

On arriving at my hotel, I rang my surveyor friend and arranged a meet tomorrow morning at my hotel and I would take him to see the site already arranged with Arthurs PA.

I was pleased with my chance meeting with Arthur and very inpatient to get working on it, as it seemed he did also. Little knowing what I would find out and experience in the coming months!

My first night at the hotel I went for my evening meal and had booked a table for one. This was very well placed, so I could see out into the garden and in the distance the car park.

It was very busy in the dinning area and tables were very full, so about twenty minutes after starting my meal I was approached by the waiter, if I would mind a lady joining me as all the other tables were full. As a joke I replied, "Certainly if she is attractive."

With a smile the waiter just raised his hand in a beckoning motion and the most attractive woman of about the same age as me, walked up. I staggered up to hold her chair for her to sit down at my table.

I then said, "My name is Bret Mann and I'm pleased to meet you." She smiled a smile that really didn't need her to spoil it, by saying in a very thick accent, "mines Eliza, me pleased to meet you."

I gulped and replied, "Do you speak very much English?"

A frown and she replied, "no- not really" and shaking her head in a no.

Thus, I enjoyed the meal and company giggling, and helping Eliza make a conversation.

She was very careful how she spoke, and I lightened the conversation. I also said, "I had not even tried to learn another language."

I must admit, it did make me feel good and enabled me to forget everything else for the evening!

The next day, I had an early breakfast and had driven to Arthur's cabin by 9am.

My surveyor was waiting to greet me and no sooner had we said, "good morning" we all got into

Arthur's car and we were taken on a tour round the area, with him pointing out what he thought they should build, with my surveyor and myself doing the same.

We then were taken to a nearby cafe for lunch then back to the cabin after this to discuss our findings and suggestions.

Both the surveyor and I came up with the idea of brick-built chalets with small gardens. Each one detached with the plan to initially only start having people we had carefully checked on and whom would be suitable and would be able to pay a higher weekly rental. We decided to make it an exclusive site and considered that eventually, we may sell the properties to the older people as retirement homes, whilst leasing the plots they stand on. We could build a few shops and make an exclusive club house for dining and entertaining.

Arthur and I would go halves on the cost of setting this up, including all the development and staff costs.

Nearer to the beach area we would have some more shops and a club house for just non static touring caravans to visit.
We gave the job to my surveyor and asked him to

draw up plans and get planning permission. We would all meet again in one week's time at the cabin.

Arthur had invited me to dine with him at a local restaurant this evening to catch up and have a nice night out.

I returned to my hotel and as it was a warm day, got changed to go on the beach. I walked to the beach enjoying the fresh sea air.

I sat on the sun bed and under the Umbrellas. Lying down for a while just contemplating my new venture with Arthur.

My investment was not going to be a small amount, but I had every intention of making the holiday village idea work. Also, it put me back into the rental business. It was a nice position near the coast. I had been successful at making a living or more, at providing good reasonable priced living accommodation.

I asked the waiter for a gin and tonic and it came very quickly, so I sat up gazing through my binoculars around the beach and came across sitting on a sun bed near the cliff, the lady I had at my table for dinner last night.

She was in discussion with a man, who looked a bit of a tough guy with broken nose and broad shoulders, they both were arguing by the flailing of arms and hands angrily.

The man had a blazer on and made an angry gesture then walked away to be joined by another man in a blazer in a discussion.

Eliza the lady I had dinner with, put a sun hat on and lay down on the sunbed in the open taking in sun rays.

My mind was thinking why she was on her own, last night and apparently, had people with her who she knew?

I watched the men walk out the beach entrance and had the incline to ask her to join me, so I beckoned a waiter gave him a tip and asked him to go to Eliza and see if she would like to join me.
The waiter came back and said, "As far as I could understand she is happy where she is catching the rays of the sun sir."

I looked up and she was giving me a wave. I waved back and lifted my glass to her!

I continued to look around through my binoculars and wondered if I was right, the men were bodyguards. Hum, very interesting I thought!!

Through my binoculars I eventually caught a glimpse of the bodyguards still near the entrance watching Eliza. Why-o–why? I must make enquiries to find out, I thought again.

CHAPTER 2

An evening together.

The evening came and as I had arranged with Arthur he was in the taxi that picked me up when I had settled down in the front seat, I was told that he had also asked Lucy his PA and a friend of hers called Sue Moore.

I looked at him smiled and said, "You have not got the idea of fixing me up with a date have you?"

He smiled saying, "Now would I do a thing like that? He chuckled again then said, "Only joking Bret, Lucy had arranged for her to come and I wanted my PA with me so that's the reason she is coming as Lucy's friend!!"

I grinned, Replying, "That's OK then."
By this time, we had arrived at the restaurant and Lucy and her friend were waiting at the entrance door to the dining room. Introductions were made and I noticed Sue looked in her late thirties, very

attractive, well-dressed in a nice, pleated skirt and white blouse and a very pleasant smile to round it off.

The waiter took us to a well-placed table that had a good view of all the dinning area.

After we had ordered and began to drink our bottle of Merlot, I had by this time, surveyed the customers at their tables. So, I recognised the Blond Eliza, who I had dinner with in the hotel last night.

I was surprised that she was sitting with the two men who I called bodyguards and another woman who looked like she was capable of defending herself and others if necessary.

Sue, who was sitting at side of me smiling said, "You seem to be interested in the fair-haired girl on the table just across the room, are you?"

Looking round at her I shook my head in a no gesture and told her about how she was my dinner guest last night and also my observations on the beach, and how I thought they were bodyguards!

Sue chuckled and informed me to my surprise, that she is a daughter of a Russian diplomat over here in England at a university not too far away. The men and the woman are her bodyguards - as I had guessed. She cannot go anywhere without them. On her father's orders!

Arthur and Lucy were grinning like Cheshire cats together.

Arthur still smiling said to me, "Sorry I didn't mention, Sue works for MI5!"

I nearly choked drinking my wine, looking at them I said, "Then I will be careful what I say and smiled at her, and she just looked at me and raised her glass to me.

I then said to Arthur," is that woman why you are in this area then?"

Arthur smiled and answered "no comment."

I just murmured back to Sue, "All I want to know is why it was me, at my table?"

"I will ask her when I can, I speak Russian!" was her reply.

True to her word, when the ladies went to the powder room, on their return Sue said, "I spoke to

Elisa and she said she chose you to be with, because you looked honest, homely and very British" Then burst out laughing as I did too, with the others, also joining in.

We all got on very well as the evening went on and on returning to Arthur's cabin, I declined another drink to get back to my hotel. To my surprise Sue said she would go with me as she is tired and is staying at this hotel also.

We set off in the taxi back to the hotel and Sue surprised me by admitting she works in MI5 with friends of mine from the regiment and named Mike and Ray, both having been mates in the marine commando regiment.

Sue informed me, how she had a case which Ray was involved in not far from the hotel we are staying at and that Ray had got re-involved in the MI5 were he met his lady friend while working for them and continues to do so.

So, I asked her why she was interested in the blond Russian girl. Sue replied very honestly, "MI5 are always interested in diplomat's kin and keep a gentle eye on them and their bodyguards."

I looked at her and said, "A good answer, but my instincts are telling me it's a little more than that!"

I received a smile which I was beginning to like.

"Well, that's all I'm going to say, so I shall say good night" and got out the car and went into the hotel. I followed and lost her as she went through the door to the rooms. She had disappeared.

In my room I sat thinking about the evening and considered there was more going on in this area than I was aware of?

I put the TV on and had the news reports on. Made a cup of coffee and contemplated on all that had happened today.
I felt tired and went to bed and fell into a troubled sleep.

I didn't see anyone in the dinning room at breakfast so, decided to have a day out; going along the coast road and stopping where I wanted to.

After about half an hours drive I found a small chalet site with static caravans and a shop including a café and parked.It was busy with families and many young people in groups.

I went to the cafe and sat outside where they also had a seating area near to a children's area with slides, roundabouts and swings on. This had a few children on with their parents sitting close by at tables drinking hot drinks and eating cakes.

Sitting down at a table for four, I ordered a coffee and a slice of toast.

This soon came and I was eating, drinking and pensively thinking very deeply, about the blond girl and her bodyguards! Also, about Sue who worked for MI5.

I was not too sure a diplomat's daughter warranted a visit by MI5? So, what was Sue really doing in this area?

Is there more happening than I know?

Is there more to the blond girl being here, more than appears on the 'surface?'

I picked my mobile up and rang a number I rarely use!

It was answered by Mike, my old comrade in arms who now works for MI5. I explained my doubts and thoughts and after swopping pleasantries he said he would ring me back.

I left the cafe and walked down to the beach and

had a pleasant wonder along it and then returned to my parked car and drove off.

CHAPTER 3

A mystery begins.

In a large house situated on the top of the cliffs not too far away from the hotel where Bret is staying…

In a room set out like a library with books, chairs and two desks, sat two men.

The smaller man dressed very casual in cotton shirt and trousers. He had grey hair on the back and sides, with a bald patch above this. He was about five foot eight in height, with a grey beard and moustache, and thick black lenses in his glasses, which tended to hide his Chinese eyes.

He was called Fung Chow and he is the head of the Chinese secret service in Britain and Europe.
Opposite him, was a tall man in his late 50s with piercing blue eyes, grey hair, a pleasant face and black rimed glasses. He was known as Colonel Popov the Russian head of their local secret service in Briton and Europe.

Both had a whisky in front of them although it was before lunch.

Both were smoking Havana cigars with the air conditioning on and a fan sucking up the smoke being exhaled outside.

Popov was saying, "You know about the planning permission for a chalet complex applied for at the estate not far from here, I assume" his eyes meeting Fung Chow's as far as he could tell!

"Yes, my friend" he replied with a half smile and a puff of his cigar.

Popov raised his eyebrows in amazement and said, "What do you think about it?" at the same time blowing smoke out his mouth while saying it.
Fung Chow said, "Not much, too near to our local operations and we are making an approach to buying their land from the owner."

Umm "We agree and feel the same but of course being closer to us we prefer to own the land!" said Popov.

Fung Chow smiled slowly retorting, "Then it looks like we will be competing to buy it."

"Yes, that's why I invited you here to see if we could arrange a deal with you, as we have in our hands another plot of land we brought, in the area you operate from, and would offer you this if you would not compete for this area?"

Fung Chow looked at Popov, gave him a grimace changing to a smile and replied, "I'm sure I do not know the area you are thinking off, but if it would be any use to us, yes, I would make a deal"

Popov inwardly knew it was their local base as this area was to them, but if he wants to play games, I will play them as well!!

"Well, that is good then, I think we can leave the details to our people who deal with these things then? Do you want another drink before we have lunch?" Chow shook his head in a no and they both stood up as the butler came in to take them for lunch together.

So, the mystery enfolds me, without me having any idea what it will bring or how it would involve me.

I had driven further along the coast road and had now parked in a café car park I very often stopped at, to have lunch when I'm in this area.

I sat outside at a table away from anyone else and ordered my BLT sandwiches and a small gin and tonic.

My mobile phone rang and it was Mike from MI5. "Hi Bret" he began, "can we talk ok?"

"Yes, I'm in the open at a table with no one near me, its ok."

He replied, "I've had a word with 'T' about your enquiries and I can tell you why Sue is therThis all comes under the national Secrets act, so please realise it can only be repeated to one of our representatives, no one else."

I replied, "OK I understand."

Mike began, "First the land you want to develop is at the side of land owned by our friends! The Russians based in the embassy in London. Their boss is called Popov who is head of their secret services in Europe. This is why Sue is in that area at the moment trying to find out why they have this place and what is it being used for."

"I am afraid your investment to create a chalet and

touring caravan area that is at the side of their area will, I'm sure, prompt them to try and buy it from its owner, thus you and Arthur will be approached, we think, to buy the land at an extortionate price."

"It also has created an offer from the agents who buy land for the Chinese to make an offer and we understand Popov and Fung Chow the head of their secret service are meeting there today. We are sorry you are involved but would ask you to keep Sue in the picture on this what ever happens please. You have my personal phone number use it any time." Mike said, "good luck" and rang off.

I had plenty of time on my hands, so I decided to ring my surveyor dealing with my new intended investment in the proposed chalet park on my friend's land in Norfolk.

He answered very quickly and said he was surprised I had rang him as he had just finished on the phone, having been talking to the firm who are dealing with the plans and planning permission on the chalets.

They had just told him they had now had two approaches to buy the land as it is. He gave me the names and contact numbers of the people dealing with each bid and had sent a email to my partner in this venture informing him.

I asked him if the bids came to him after they had put in the plans and after they had also taken in the planning. The answer was yes.

I then rang Arthur; my friend and partner in this venture, as he is the owner of the land and his decision on any sale would have to be his.

He answered very quickly. "Hi Bret. I know what you are going to say, it's about our scheme and plans I guess. Well, my answer is no and I'm still going on with our proposed chalet area."

My reply was, "I guessed you would and you know I'm with you, but it's so quick and by the look of it a high price is offered. I'm going to investigate this a little more. OK with you?"

"Yes, OK no problem you have my phone number I'm on a trip aboard for a week. I will catch up on my return, you have my PAs number as well, good luck!"

I then rang Sue and asked her to meet me on the hotels beach, in a hour.

On the beach I found two sun beds in a isolated

spot and paid for their use. Sitting there on my own I sat and contemplated my next action on the problem of the chalet area.

It wasn't long before Sue tuned up looking very nice in shirt and jeans. I asked her to sit opposite me. Ordered two gin and tonics and by the time I had asked Sue if Mike had contacted her, the drinks came.

After a sip of mine I looked into her eyes and said to her, "Sue I intend to investigate the two offers from the Russians and Chinese and try and find out why they want the land. Will you work with me?"

Her smile and intent showed as she looked in my eyes she replied, "Yes I will, as I was going to ask you if we could work together!"

I gave her a very bright, pleased smile and said, "That's great. Would you tell me what you have found out that I can be told?"

She nodded yes and began to give me the gist of her findings.

"MI5 had discovered that Popov through agents, had bought the house and the land adjourning Arthurs, land. So, I have been trying to find out why."

"Our drones had shown up training areas in unarmed combat and thus the assumption is it's being used as a training area for their agents."

"You may wonder why Norfolk? And this reason we do not know. I also know his opposite number from the Chinese embassy is visiting him at the moment. This we assume is to get an agreement for them not to oppose him buying the land as he would not like it having the Chinese on his doorstep either. That's it I'm afraid, so the suggestion is, we become on the surface friends and maybe get an invite to one of his dinners and find out more!"

I replied, "Yes, I agree to work with you to do this but also I will let my agents dealing with the proposed deal from Popov to let him know. I would like to see him and talk about the sale. This may give us a chance to get in the house and see what we can find out."

I then picked up the phone and rang my agents dealing with it to do this.

Popov was sitting at the desk in the library area when the intercom buzzed and he flicked the switch saying, "yes?" "Just had a phone call from the agents dealing with the land adjoining us saying, one of the investors in this project, would like to see you informally," said a female voice.

"Invite him and his partner tonight. I don't have anyone attending who does not know the rules" Patrov flicked the switch off and picked up his cigar case and lit a Havana, looking very happy with a wide smile on his face thinking! So, the canary is coming to the cat Umm…

CHAPTER 4

The investigation dinner.

I was sitting with a cup of tea on Sue's veranda discussing our cover and our plan to get information on the reason the Russians had acquired the house and the reason and purpose they were now using it for.

Sue had also told me the layout and use it had been designed for when it was taken over by the secret service on another case she was associated with. Also it's use then was about terrorism, as it had the facilities from the sea land and air to train and coordinate a terrorist attack, but she did not think that was the Russians aim at the moment as there are plenty of other groups trying to organise terrorism.

Having been told this I looked at her and gave a grimace and continued saying, "Sue we will be in great danger entering the lions den together and no doubt you have checked my past experience on covert missions with your colleagues who work with you at MI5. So I have no worry about my capabilities, but I have not the authority deal with anything they throw at me!"

She smiled and said, "You are now from today a temporary agent of MI5 and I will loan you a fire arm as well."

Sue looked at me and with a serious expression said, "Bret I have become very fond of you. I feel because of this, I should let you know the position you are going tobe in through doing this. This is a dangerous game, and we will be dealing with the head of the Russian secret service in England, who is a very dangerous man and has a lot of resources to call on if required to do so and who would not think twice about having you killed?"

I just said, "Well it's about time someone did something!!"

She smiled shaking her head and replied, "Right let's go for it" and handed me a gun and case and I left the room to get changed into my dinner attire, then to go to the hotel reception to await our taxi.

Popov was in the process of dressing for dinner and as doing so, his mind was occupied with thoughts of his guest this evening.

He had got his people to check on Bret and found out after a very good career in the armed forces, he had bought property and after selling them to a large concern, he had made a small fortune to invest as he wished. So, no doubt Bret thought investing in a chalet park a good risk, a typical capitalist! This made him someone he could maybe use.

The colonel's phone rang and he answered it saying, "I will be down in ten minutes, put them in the library for drinks."

He tied his bow tie and looked at himself in the mirror thinking this is going to be an interesting evening.
While waiting in reception, Sue surprised me by explaining how she had in the past, had a case of political asylum people who rented a place not far away from the house they were going to.

She also mentioned how Ray Marriot, who is a friend of mine from the forces, was also involved and was very grief stricken by the loss of his lady friend by a sniper who was the sister of the man who owned the house near by. They could not prove it but they all think it was 'Popov' who had arranged the sniper kill to her.

I looked at her and said, "What you have just told me makes me, more determined to do this investigation."

Suddenly a voice said to them, "Sir and madam your taxi is waiting."

We both looked up recognising the voice and it was my old friend Ray Marriot, standing there in a peaked cap smiling at us! We just walked to the taxi and got in.

As he started the car he said, "I heard from Mike we were investigating Popov? So, I have wangled my cases so I can come and give you two a hand as I have a personal interest in doing so! By the way, this moustache is a false one for tonight's driver image."

We both smiled and I said, "Ray you are a sight for sore eyes and welcome."

Sue nodded her agreement.

It didn't take long to get to the house and Ray opened the doors for us to enter the large hallway, having been greeted by a very well-built butler.

I looked around the hall entrance area it had 6

doors leading off it, a coat and hat stand and stairs on the right leading, I assumed, to the bedrooms.

At the end door on the right a big male who looked like a boxer or bodyguard stood ready to see us into the room that looked very much like a library with walls full of books and tall steps to get to the higher shelves, were tucked away in the corner.
We had taken off our coats and joined the congregating people standing about talking with drinks they had been supplied with by waiters circulating around the room.

I stopped a waiter passing by with an empty tray in his hands, saying, "could you bring us two gin and tonics please?"

I looked at Sue who smiled saying softly, "it looks like we are to be accosted by some one!" nodding towards a small man dressed in a Russian captain's dress uniform.

He bowed his head and in very good English said, "May I introduce myself." Bowing his head he continued, "Colonel Popov asked me to guide you and take care of you this evening."

Sue smiling said to him, "we would be grateful if you do. As we both have not ever been to your dinners before, first let me introduce us. "I am Sue and my partner is Bret!"

He graciously replied, "Captain Kinsky, of the second parachute regiment."

Shaking hands I said, "Bret Mann ex- major in the British second Para regiment." He stood at attention acknowledging my rank. Then said to us "please follow me" bowing to Sue, who said softly to me smiling, "Well done he thought he could be overbearing, but your rank has made him more respectful."

We followed him arm in arm.

Ray had parked the car in his allotted space and walked back to the front door. He was told he could get tea and refreshments in the building they had arranged for drivers to wait in, where they could stay all night until they were called to take their people back home. It was chosen to be near and within easy reach for when they were required.

It was a reasonable size place with staff serving behind a large long bar with tea, coffee and water to drink. Also sandwiches of many different fillings were on offer.

He opted for a tea and salad roll, that he carried to a

small table on a tray in the corner of the room.

He sat down and looked around the room, ther were some drivers, and he guessed a good few Russian bully boys to watch the people who enter the area.

One of the drivers came and introduced himself. Named Joe, he informed them he was a local MPs driver for the evening.

Ray soon found out the MP person was a woman in the labour party, who frequented the dinners provided by the Russian colonel Popov.

Soon they joined others and Ray had a gist of the people attending the dinner from the local area or on holiday in this area.

Ray noticed when he went outside for fresh air that there was a path towards the sea. He asked if he was ok to walk down the path, having noticed a bench seat he could sit on it. He was not to go any further as he was warned not to disappear out of sight, and he assured them he would not.

On arriving at the bench, he sat down and did a cursory search for bugs, which he did not find, so sat down looking out to sea. It was a nice warm evening with the waves braking on the rocks, nearby.

Ray pressed on his top pocket in which he had a small radio and put a very small plug in his ear. His earpiece in, he said quietly into his cuff link, "Sun Ray here, do you receive, over?"

A crackle then Mike's voice came on saying, "M, here receiving ok. Any luck Sun Ray?"

"No luck, security too tight, I can hardly move so many of them around, over."

"T thinks we need some people inside. It is very suspicious why the sudden move to the Norfolk area and I agree, over" replied Mike.

"Will keep trying, hope the other two are getting results, Sun Ray, over and out."

Ray sat back pondering the same as Mike had. He then stood up looked round and slowly walked back to the parking area.

Arriving back in the area where the cars were parked, Ray walked over to a driver polishing his maroon Jaguar. As he approached the man doing this turned and said to him, "Hi had a nice walk? You will not get many places here that are not bugged or without security about, typically, Russian!"

"You been here before then?" asked Ray.

"Yep twice now" came back his reply, as he turned around putting his hand out saying, "Hi Bills my name."

"Ray" he replied, shaking his hand. "Who have you brought here?"

"Well, I work for a hire firm, and today I brought the Chinese delegation, who are staying only a few miles away. The areas got more foreigners than locals now, Bill continued saying.

Ray smiled and said, "Yes it does seem strange the Ivan's and Orientals are so friendly!"

Bill said, "The Reds have got this place, and I heard the Chinese are interested in the area adjoining, or so I understand."
Ray replied, "I didn't know they were that friendly?"

At that moment Bills phone rang and Ray patted his shoulder and walked on thinking, "I've got a hunch there is more to meet the eye than we know of?" He continued walking to his car.

CHAPTER 5

A dinner and approach.

Sue and I were guided to our seats at the head table near to where Popov sat, seated at the top with his wife, a rather well made lady.

Sue and I were on the right side at the corner. I sat the nearest to him then Sue and at side of her was Captain Kinsky.

It all began with the toast to the Soviet Union by Popov. Then a toast to congratulate the acquisition of a new training area and to the mayor of the local area. This was followed by the starter and the meal began.

Popov was a good host and was just attentive enough to Sue and I to be polite.
It was not until the meal finished and we had retired to another room with tables set out and wine and drinks a plenty, did he invite us to sit with his party. He opened the conversation with

me about selling the adjoining land to him.

He was very polite but firm and did not mince his words.

He began by intimating he would like the land in question as it would give him a chance of having another area to allow entrance to his land from the road and also to give him more areas of recreation, which he indicated, was the main purpose of having a branch in this area, for their employees.

He continued to try to convince me it was an area they wanted to relax, swim and be completely secure to do this in.

I let him ramble on knowing enough about the Russians and him to know he was fabricating a story to give the impression of just wanting a place by the sea to relax in.

I did remind him my interest was investment with my friend who actually owned it.

He calmly remarked he thought my friend would do what I thought was the best for them.

We were interrupted by an army officer in uniform and after a quick talk and nodding his head, came back over and apologised; he had to go as something urgent needed his attention, but asked me to think about what he had said. He left.

Sue and I circulated but did not gain any information on the new Russian-style recreation area they had created.

Sue suggested we get back to our hotel and do a report to Mike at MI5 and see if Sun Ray had got on any better.

Ray brought the car to the front entrance and goodbye was made by Kinsky and we drove off.

In the car Ray said the same had happened to him he said, "Everything's a very well guarded closed book" smiling wryly.
We arrived at the hotel and Sun Ray drove off. Sue and I said our goodbyes and went straight to our rooms.

Arriving at my room, I entered and took of my coat and tie, which I put on the chair, took off my shoes, and put all the pillows at the headboard. I sat just looking at the ceiling thinking about the evening. I had my iPad and did an email to Mike at MI5.

Early next morning I awoke, still fully dressed from the following night. I got up made a cup of tea and took it into the bathroom to drink. Then showered, shaved and put on my clothes for the day, all cotton, short sleeve shirt, chinos and socks. I had another cup of tea and then I walked down to the dinning room for breakfast.

I was directed to a table and was starting my cereal when a female voice said, "Would you mind if I join you Bret?"

I looked around smiling, recognising the voice, saying, "Of course Sue, join me with pleasure."
She put her hand bag and cardigan on a chair saying. "excuse me Bret, I will get some cereal and would you order me a tea please?"

She then walked towards the table with the breakfast cereals on to chose from.

I suddenly thought how she was a very attractive lady.

A couple of minutes went by, and she returned and sat down to eat her corn flakes.

I said to her, "You look very refreshed and perky this morning you must have slept well?"

She smiled putting milk and sugar on her cereal and replied, "Not really. I was up late in conversation with MI5 who are on a top alert due to the news coming from Ukraine of a possible invasion."

I looked at her seriously and replying. "Yes, worrying and very dangerous. I assume the secret service would be very much involved if they do invade!!"
Her face became very grim and she said, "We are involved and it's already put a different meaning to the land the Russians have just acquired here and that means a different approach. I will be going back to London as soon as I am ready and should return this evening."

I shook my head saying, "then we better get together and talk then."

She nodded her head in a yes.

I had decided to go along the coast and look at a chalet site I had visited before, to give me an idea of the layout of sites in the area.

I arrived and was walking around the site when my mobile rang.

It was Mike of MI5 who began by telling me the Russians were on the move in Ukraine and an invasion was to begin.

This now put a different position on the Russian site where I had dinner last night, as the UK and others are now in the process of making sanctions on them and it will include probably confiscating this land from them.

I decided to return home and cut short my trip, which I was enjoying in my own way.

I had left a message at the reception for Sue and set off in the bright sunshine.

CHAPTER 6

A strange twist.

Having had a phone call from Mike arranging a meeting with T on the Monday after my return from the East coast, I travelled to London on the Sunday and booked a hotel room not far from the MI5 headquarters.

The previous evening, a note had been left at reception by Mike inviting me to a dinner on the Sunday evening. A car would pick me up at 7pm to take me to the destination arranged by him.

I was dressed for dinner in a lounge suit, sitting on a cosy chair, reading several leaflets off a rack near by, of places to visit in London.

I was suddenly disturbed by a voice I recognised as Rays, my old mate from the forces saying, "Your car is waiting sir! My name is Sun Ray" with a big grin on his face.

I looked at him myself grinning also, saying, "Hello Sun Ray, lead the way." We both left the hotel and got into the black limousine parked at the front entrance.

By now, I was not surprised at seeing Ray driving it, he seemed to be working on this case.

He slowly pulled away from the hotel entrance, looking in the mirror saying to me "I am dealing with your case of the land sale, and I have just been notified that your friend Arthur is missing.
He was in a private plane owned by a friend and was flying to Canada to meet a man interested in having his company build a site there.

No wreckage has been found anywhere and they now presumed, they are all dead and arrangements are being made to sort out whom his finances and immense fortune has been left too in whatever the will states, which is being read on Wednesday next week."
I was shaken and for a few seconds could not reply, but my mind was busy thinking about what to do next.

I stuttered saying, "That's a shock, who is dealing with his estate etc?"

Ray replied, "A firm in London called William Brown Solicitors and you may have an invite to it waiting in your home?"

"I will get my PA to check, who picks up my mail while I'm away."

I picked up my mobile and phoned her.

She answered very quickly, listened to my request about a letter from a legal firm and replied, "Yes I have one stating they request your attendance at a reading of Arthurs will at 11am in London next week."

I replied, "confirm I will attend, please. Many thanks speak later" I put the mobile back in my pocket, pondering on why they wanted me to attend.
I said to Ray. "Looks like it may be an interesting read of the will I'm puzzled about it!!"

He jokingly said, "Maybe he's left his fortune to you?" Half-smiling, I said, "some hope" and then sat there sadly thinking about my deceased friend.

Arriving at our destination, I got out and Ray drove the car to the parking area and I stood waiting for him. He was back in five minutes. We were both taken to a room and shown in the door.

I was blinking my eyes as it was very well lit, and we both were led by a waiter to a small bar in the right corner and offered a drink. I ordered a Gin and tonic and Ray said, "make that two" to the bar tender.

As we toasted to Arthur, a voice behind us said, "Don't forget me - the same for me" Mike had arrived.

We turned and shook hands giggling, all greeting each other as we were brothers in arms from our past, forces experiences.
Mike said, opening his arms in a gesture embracing the room saying, "This is 'T's personal dinner room for entertaining the important clients he meets, so we are honoured to be allowed it to dine in.

I commented that we were and continued "but I always knew he recognised his best agents - you two!"

I raised my glass to them and they raised it to each other saying together, "of course he does!"

We all sat down in the easy chairs and began to reminisce. Within 10 minutes we were asked by the waiter to take our seats at the table.

We sat at the table making comments throughout the first course, on missions we had done in the forces together, making funny comments on certain escapades and what we did in them.

For the second course we had beef and all the trimmings with Yorkshire puds and nice gravy. Mikes comment was, "Like my mothers Sunday lunch and the gravy is as good, don't you think?"

The other two with their mouths full, just nodded yes.

Then Mike continued to say, "well to change the subject I need to put you both in the MI5s position of the Russians land. We have to confiscate the land that you and Arthur were to develop."

'T' had expressed an opinion as to our next steps. Mike intimated to us that they had found a lot of information and military equipment Russians had started to accumulate there. Also, the government had instructed the MI5 and MI6 departments to use it and keep tight security on it.

'T' had also told Mike he would, if required, get MI5 backing if I tried to investigate my now demised friend Arthur's death, as it may have Russian connections.

Mike continued, "Unfortunately, 'T' has to cancel tomorrow's meeting, but he is keeping Sue and Ray on the case to help you."

I looked at him with a slight smile on my face and said, "I did wonder why we had been given T's dinning room this evening."
However, I welcomed the help offered by Ray and Sue and suggested that maybe a meet could happen next week after I had been to the will reading.

Mike with a smug smile on his face replied, "I knew you would, but as you know that's 'T'.

Ray then commented he looked forward to our working together.

The meal went on in good spirits and a lot of reminiscing on our past was enjoyed.

We all said our cheerio's, saying we must do this again soon and Mike went back to work. Ray and I left and were shaking hands at the door of my hotel minutes later.

CHAPTER 7

My life changes.

The date for the will reading arrived. It was a change of weather, as it was raining heavily on my journey in a taxi to the solicitors. I was tired and had been late in my bed the previous night and was still half asleep from eating good food and plenty of wine with a friend I had not seen for a few years.

The last two days had gone very quickly and now it was Wednesday, which had come with a wet start, meaning I had to get a taxi to the solicitors. Even a brolly did not stop me getting wet whilst I was just walking to the door.

I was just shaking the rain of my brolly and started to walk towards the desk when a female voice said, "excuse me are you Mr. Bret Mann?"
I turned and smiled at a very attractive young lady standing in the doorway and continued by saying, "Yes I am."

"This way, please follow me" she replied. I certainly thought it was a very nice walk following her.

I was shown by her to a medium sized room with a large desk and asked to sit in a seat near the desk.

I nodded to the male sitting near to me and gave the lady who had shown me to it, a big nod and smile which was returned. I sat down.

I had informed the solicitors dealing with the will that I would attend with my solicitor and friend named Bill Noon who had been my solicitor since I first started in business. I trusted his firm completely.

He was guided to the chair next to me. I stood up and shook hands as he did and he looked at me smiling, saying to me, "good to see you again Bret."

I nodded my head in a yes and smiled.

A middle-aged male behind the desk introduced himself as William Brown junior, and he began to read the will.

He quickly read out the legal bits making his firm executors. The first part after this, was the money gifts to certain employees including the old man and woman, who looked after his home and also the cottage where they lived. He had left them £50,000.

They sat at the other side near the desk corner. The older lady, burst into tears. The young woman who was close by put her arm around her, to comfort her.

Then Will Brown Junior dropped the bombshell, announcing that the rest of Arthur's fortune, shares, property and holdings were left to me!!

I sat there stunned, nonplussed, my solicitor Bill took my hand shaking it saying, "Well done you are very rich now!"

I looked at him and could not initially get my voice working and when I did, I stuttered, "why me I wonder?"

He replied, "He has no living relatives or family so he must have thought a lot of you?" Then shrugged his shoulders and walked away.

I looked around the room at other faces. Some were smiling as though they were pleased, and two others were definitely not very pleased. I found out later they were people who had got to know him personally and hoped he may have left them something in his will!!

Following the meeting, one male, who was dressed very well in a navy suit, introduced himself as Brian, Chief executive of the building company saying, "My name's Brian Welsh and anytime you wish to see me and discuss the future, please do so and the sooner the better."

By now I had gained my sanity back and replied, "I will do that as soon as I can, but I have to see my PA and get it sorted on my calendar." I could see we would get on and he nodded a yes and went...
Several people came up and introduced themselves and shook my hand, but by now I just wanted to get away and talk and plan my future actions. So I went to my solicitor and we left together in a taxi to his office not too far away.

As we went in the reception, he told a lady behind the desk he wanted tea for two in his office and did not want to be interrupted if possible.

The tea came and he sat at his desk with me facing him.

He took a drink from his cup and sat back saying, "Well my friend I can imaging its all been a shock and will take a while to get it sorted in your mind I expect?"

Smiling at him I said, "Funny thing it is a surprise and shock, but I intend not to let anyone down and will take my time, to make sure I don't.
I want your firm to deal with all the legal work and watch my back. When you cannot get me, I have a very good PA - as you know. Let me know when things are sorted, and I will contact the chief executive and go and see him to get the gist of what's happening."
He nodded, yes and we were deep in talk for a time, of what it entails and how he would sort out the necessary items I did need to bother with.

He then was surprised when I said, "I am not happy with the short investigation of how the plane had disappeared and my friend had died and I will be making my own investigation, with help, to at least be satisfied enough to rest my mind. This would entail me being away for a while and I will need to leave the necessary cover from himself on the business and legal side. Then I intend to go on my friend's last journey to Canada and see what I can find out."

I took another sip of tea and smiled when I also said, "After all I'm rich enough to do so!"

He then, on finishing our talk, said, "Ok, give me a week and I should have the legal work in place, so I suggest you see the firms CEO as soon as you can."

We shook hands and I left to go to my offices to give them the news!!
When I got back to the office I rang Mike at MI5, who answered the phone.

He was given the facts on my inheritance as I knew them and my intentions of checking my friend's death more thoroughly, also my thoughts that it may have been associated with our "red comrades" on the land adjourning that is now mine.

He answered by saying, "Well I think we can help you there as we also now have a greater interest in what they are up to. Congratulations Bret and give me a day or so and I will let you know, must go bye."

Knowing that's the answer I expected, I then called my staff to the office and told them the news. To assure them it will mean business as usual in the firm they are all working in.

I just settled down to a cup of tea when my mobile rang and a voice saying, "Hi Bret, Sun Ray here."

I replied saying, "Hi Ray, are you still on the case of the Russians?"

He chuckled replying, "Yep I sure am partner" in a poor American accent.

He then said "Well on this phone I can only say our interest now is because Russian sanctions have started, this will include their place and property on that land. Also, I will be on my usual number if you require any help at all."

"Thanks Ray that's good news" I replied.

"Ok over and out" and the phone call was finished.

'Hum', I thought this could get interesting!! I then rang the CEOs PA to arrange a meeting with him and myself asap.

The next few days went by very quickly, with the week ending at the builder firms' offices with the CEO and in the first place a board meeting to elect a new chair of the group. Being the main shareholder, they elected me as chair and as that was all the business for this meeting, they all left having introduced themselves apart from Mary Sherwood, who was vice chair they had elected last time.

The three of us plus the CEO's PA were taken to the chairs special dinning room on the top floor. It was a very nicely set out and could cater for up to fifty guests if needed and the chef in the kitchen, I was told had catered for that many times before, when it was necessary.

The waiter was in a dinner suit and tie. I thought to myself when he began to take orders, I've certainly gone up in the world now.

We were asked if we wanted wine and they all looked at me and I said, "I do not but if others would like some please be free to do so as I have a lot to do, and wine could fuddle the brain!"

They all laughed, and each one said, "me neither."

The CEO did most of the talking on and about the business on which, I asked questions and got satisfactory answers.
I then turned the conversation to my intention of investigating my friend's death and they both looked surprised, but understood my explanation as to why I wanted to do it.

I asked Mary, if she would mind holding the reins a bit longer and told them both, they could contact me through my PA any time night or day.

I drove back to my office and on the way, thought I had a car following me but I turned a few corners to shake him and I did.

Ah well I thought, you may be imagining things, but its best to be safe than sorry.

After sorting out a few days absence and the things that needed attention with my PA who had just left, my phone rang, it was my friend Mike in MI5.

He said, "Bret we have gone into the land at the side of yours on the east coast and we have found quite an armoury and other things, so is it possible you could come tomorrow lunch about 12 noon as 'T' would like to see you?"
I replied, "Yes see you then, by the way I seem to have a car following me, or I thought it was?"

"Was it a green Rover?" he replied.

"Yes it was"I responded back.

He chuckled and retorted, "I will tell you tomorrow why" and cut off.

Umm I thought as much, it could be MI5 then! This

conversation started me to wonder if MI5 had an interest of involving me in a case I'm connected to unknowingly in some way, I had not realised I was?

I went to sleep this night puzzled and yet very interested to find out what it was.

I awoke early and had a breakfast of cereal and toast and a cup of tea. Showered, shaved, and dressed in a suit.

Taking a look at my newspapers that had been delivered, they were full of the Russians invading Ukraine, the UKs support and what they intend to supply them in arms.
I contacted my PA and gave her my jobs I wanted her to do and where I was going for lunch.

I made several phone calls and by this time it was 11am and my phone rang, informing a car was waiting for me.

I went down and as I expected, Sun Ray was driving it, I got in and we set off to a meeting and adventure that would change my life in the future!

CHAPTER 8

The beginning of the adventure.

Sun Ray and I walked into MI5 and I got my visitors badge and we were shown to 'Ts' dining room. This time, the head of the table was the only one set with cutlery and napkins etc.

Mike was waiting for us, and we were directed to our chairs by the waiter and asked if we wanted a drink, to which we all replied not yet and thanks.

Mike informed us 'T' would be only a few minutes as he had a minister with him whose responsibility included MI5 and MI6, a army General from the Ministry of Defence, and two ladies - one was a police representative and the other a PA to 'T'.
They all came in, were seated and introductions made with the reminder we were all under the secrets act in the room.

The minister gave a toast to the King, and we

began our starters with 'Ts' guests. The three of us sat opposite them.

'T' began to give everyone a brief rundown explaining how "now with Russia and the sanctions being levied on them, we have to consider every item we can, that has been confiscated from the comrades and has a use for terrorism and could be used in a war over here."

He continued by saying, "We have found many items and papers that proves this land was to be used for this effect in our country, so we must follow up any leads we have to get rid of this threat."

Mike then gave a quick resume of items and organisations that were connected in some way or other to the Russians.

With all this in mind and my involvement already. On the east coast with Sun Ray and Mike, they would like me to continue working with them to discover who the organisation was who would implement the plans they had for the UK.

I replied that I would like to know this myself and I would help in any way I can, as I can make the time in my position to do so.

After the meal we all went to the room were they had after dinner drinks and 'T' said to me, "Thanks Bret, I thought you would like to get involved, and I've made arrangements for you to get an MI5 pass etc, also a pass to carry a firearm, plus Sue will become you girlfriend and partner. Are you happy with this?"

I smiled and said, "yes, I will be only too glad to have such a team with me. I guess it will take me a couple of days to sort my end out."

He then retorted, "Bret from the time you leave here you will be under MI5 scrutiny and protection, and you go no where in a car except the one with Sun Ray as the driver."

I nodded a yes and he went off to talk to the MP. Mike and Ray came over and Mike said, "Bret don't get too worried by all the do's and don'ts etc. it will be no different than when you helped us out going to the Russians dinner and the contacts you made, plus Sue and Ray will be there to help."

I smiled saying, "No need to do a new will then?"

Ray jokingly replied, "not unless you want us in it, I reckon." We all had a giggle together and the meeting finished. As T left, Ray and I went to our car, picking up my passes from the reception area. Ray drove back to my hotel arranging to pick me up to go to the office at 9am.

I went to my room and had a disturbed sleep with my mind going from one thing to the other and awoke still tired.

A shave and shower and I felt ready for the day ahead.

During breakfast my mind kept straying to the next part of my life I had committed myself to do. Maybe I should have said I'm ok as I am? Maybe I was a bit too quick in saying I would help MI5? Then I argued with myself - I should try and find out for my friend who died. Plus I did take an oath in the forces for king and country.

Eventually I came to the conclusion I needed to do it for my own sake and help my friends and country. Then I just put out of my mind any doubts and eagerly looked forward to the adventure ahead.

I was ready and eager to get started by the time Ray arrived to collect me in his car and was very jovial on the way to MI5.

I was taken to different departments to get my information and identity cards. I then signed for a firearm and holster, plus a phone, and then spent time with an expert on firearms and other things. Then I bumped into Ray who took me for lunch.

During the lite lunch Ray told me he was following a lead that may give us a name for who else was involved with Popov in the use of the land and base.
He said, "I wonder if you would like to come along and see what transpires"? I nodded yes.

So, he got the car and we set off to a place in London town that was a sort of men's only club and dropped me of at the front entrance, while he parked the car.

The door man who was just inside the entrance door, politely asked if he could help and I told him I was waiting outside for a friend.

I stood waiting and not paying much attention to people going by until a tall male came up and asked me the time.

I said, "2 o'clock."

He looked at me standing in front of me and said,

"do as I say you have a gun pointed at you." He then put his hand behind him and gave a signal and a car drew up. He opened the door and shoved me into the back. He went to the front seat beside the other person who was driving. He turned round and showed me his gun and said, "take it easy and you will not be hurt."

As I fell on the seat I had the forethought to press the emergency button on my phone from MI5.

The tall man kept his eyes on me but as long as they don't find the phone MI5 should trace it easily, or so I hoped.

The car stopped in a garage and knowing they would search me I pushed the phone in the seam of the back seat and got out.

CHAPTER 9

The chase starts.

Ray had just found a parking space when Bret's emergency button must have been pressed, setting an alarm off on his phone and his car radio, which came through as he restarted it, showing the direction to where the phone was on a small screen. He had no hesitation and shot out quickly onto the road back to where he had left Bret.

Arriving at the last place he left him, he jumped out and shouted to the man attending the door, asking if he had seen the man he left at the entrance. The doorman replied that he went off in a black top rover car, five minutes ago.

Ray set off following the position appearing on the navigation screen, with his lights flashing and taking risks to overtake he would not do normally.

Sue came on the radio saying, "Ray I'm on the way following the signal."

Ray replied, "Only 5 minutes since I left him."

He then picked his mic up and gave headquarters an emergency bulletin to look for a black top green rover car on the way out of London centre.

By the time he had travelled a short way up the ring road, it had stopped but the signal was still working.

Ray said aloud, "I hope it has not been thrown out the car," gritted his teeth and put his foot down.

He soon came up to the house with iron gates. Parking the car nearby in a lay by.

By the time he had walked back to the iron gates ,he was joined by two other cars. One with Sue in. She got out and quickly joined him saying, "looks like Bret has left the phone in the car!"
Next minute another car drew up and Mike got out and joined the two of them saying, "I'm giving instructions to the other men to surround the house, no-one is allowed in or out." They all understood and disappeared.

A man of medium height came up to Mike and said, "The wall is not wired but has glass cemented in on top, but there is a tree further along from here I could, with help, get on the overhanging branch and if I take some kit with me can get you pictures of doors etc, back and front before we all go in."

Mike replied, "Go to it Fred" and Fred ran off to get it done.

Ray and Sue had heard this exchange, and both were aware what was happening.

Bret was taken from the car into the house by the man who had a gun pointed at him. He was taken to a library with a big window and desk, plus books and filing cabinets galore.

He took his coat off on the man's demand and was searched. Finding his firearm and personal phone in the process, they were put in a drawer in the desk. Then he was told to sit in a chair, put his arms behind him and his wrists were tied.

The man then left the room.

I sat quietly contemplating my situation. I guessed if my MI5 emergency phone had worked MI5 should be here by now.

Outside the wall, they were getting pictures on the

car radios from Fred, and they had not seen more than three men about the place at the moment.

Mike said to Ray, "Not sure what's happening as I would have expected more people about by now but, I think the safety of Bret is paramount so I feel we must go in and try and capture and interrogate these men. I have given instructions to keep all the ground covered outside the fence in case one tries to do a runner."

Sue said, "I don't think they have seen me, so why don't I go to the gate and announce I'm lost, and could they help me?"

"Umm" said Mike, "I suppose it might work and the others could get in while you keep them occupied. Go for it Sue".

She walked to her car and drove up to the gate. Got out and pressed the intercom button.

A male's face came on the screen, and she informed them of her position and that she was exhausted.

Tom was the man who answered, and he was the man with the gun. He replied, "Well dear, I can show you the map and give you directions if you want and even make you a cup of tea. If you wish?"

Ray nudged Mike whispering with a grin, "He's fell for it."

The gates opened for Sue's car, and she slowly went in with men either side getting in at the same time. She drove to the front door and rang the bell.

Tom came to the door smiling at her and invited her inside. He guided her to a room. It looked like a lounge area with a settee that was set out as a work room used by a secretary. It had a desk with papers on it, plus a few chairs.

Sue sat at front of the desk and Tom sat at the desk opposite her.

A knock and another man walked in with a tray with tea on and asked her how she liked her tea.

She just said, "a little milk and no, sugar, please.

They were given their teas and as they all took a sip of it the door burst open, and Mike and Ray came into the room showing their passes to the men. They both put their hands up. There were another two other agents who cuffed them.

Next minute Bret came in with another agent and

Mike asked him if he was ok.

Bret said, "They have searched me but have not questioned me yet."
Mike instructed the agents to take the men to headquarters to question them and tell the rest to search the place."

Ray and I went around the house and decided the search was best left to the others and he would take me back to my place to get fresh clothes and wash.

I soon did this, then Ray took me to MI5 to write a report and discuss why they must have kidnapped me.

We went to an office after a doctor examined me and gave me the ok.

Arriving at MI5 had put me right back in the position of finding out why I had been abducted. I was told by Mike the information they had now got from their searching and interrogation, pointed to trying to dispense with me as the new owner of the land. 'Popov' wanted to completely make his area secure, from anyone entering his facility unaware of them, as his plans were to make it a secure base for agents

and military to use for the eventual access to anywhere in the UK.
Popov had already got a good way to building the area towards this purpose. With land and sea bringing the possibility of air on the land I now owned.

He had employed a hit man called Grant who they had tried to find all over the world, but so far, they have not succeeded in finding him. He is what they called an 'eliminator,' and he was good, but expensive. They also know he is an American. Even the two they captured had never seen him.

Mike said, "I'm sorry Bret. But we think the best way to draw this Grant out, is to use you as bait. We know you are a good few years older now since you have helped us before, but we feel you could cope and you will never be on your own at any time, even at night one of us will be with you."

I grimaced and replied, "I know you will do your best but, if he is as good as you say, he may find a way. However, I agree it is the only chance we have at the moment and I'm willing to try. If he is the one I encountered before, I owe him one."
Mike smiled and quipped "I thought you would." Patting me on my shoulder "Let's go then."

CHAPTER 10

So it begins.

Travelling in a taxi down a road in London it was occupied by a tall grey eyed handsome man called Grant Jr. He sat looking out the window, but his mind was preoccupied, thinking of his job now, having had a call his target had got away!

He was the son of the original eliminator who MI5 had themselves, eliminated a few years back by an agent called Ray Marriot.

So, this was a chance to cross swords with him as well, but he must be careful and concentrate on his job he was to be handsomely paid to do.

He said to the driver, "Drop me off along here thanks I've changed my mind."

He walked along, until he came to a small café he had been to several times. Went in and ordered coffee and sat down in his usual place at the end of the tables, near a front window, he could see who and what passes by.

Sitting there he was bought his coffee and he sat looking outside at the traffic and passing people, thinking what's my best way to get this contract finished so I can go back home.

*

There were computer screens on every wall and sometimes Mike put his code in a machine and it showed the face of the man they called the 'eliminator', saying, "We dealt with him a few years back; he was called Grant. Strangely, I was told only yesterday his son Grant Jr was over here!"

He looked towards another man, "Roy you were on that case."

Roy stuttered, "but I shot and killed his father and I guess Jr must have took the business over then?"

Mike then sat down and said, "Let's think on this a moment," then outloud he said, "if we follow him successfully ,we must have a plan to get him somewhere, to bait a trap for him to make a move on Bret. You Roy do not let Bret out of your or other agents sight at any time. Just force him to show his hand which we will jump on immediately. Here's what I think we should do."

An agent who was on duty happened to be near the café with Grant in. He looked at Grant thinking he had seen him somewhere, so when he arrived back in his car, he tapped the computer to look at male faces and as luck had it, he brought the old Eliminator, Grants face up.

He rang Mike and told him he had seen a dead ringer of Grant senior in the café. Mikes voice went to a higher pitch saying, "You stay with him and keep him in sight. If he moves, follow. I will send more agents we must not lose him."

I was sent to the cafe Grant was in, with Sue and sat a good way from Grant, but could see him and be ready for any move he might make.

Grant watched, Bret and Sue enter the café, sit at a table and order a drink. He also observed neither were looking round waiting for anyone. In fact, they seemed very attentive to each other, talking very seriously about something! He pondered whether to make a move or be patient and wait and see.

Grant decided to wait to see if anyone else joined them. If no one does, then he was going to make a move when or if Bret goes to the men's room. He tried to lip read but could not.

He waited 10 minutes and decided to hope Bret would make a move it would make it easy for him.

I stood up after saying to Sue to contact and say I was going to the men's room. She did!

As I slowly walked to the men's room and went in. I turned and walked towards the hand basins and I heard the door open. I looked sideways and it was Grant walking in towards a urinal.

I heard someone come in the room and walk to a toilet. Closed the door and a rustle of clothing.
Grant had walked to the wash basin next to me and said as he got there, "Nice weather isn't it?"
I turned looked at him and replied, "Very good for the time of year."

He then turned and dried his hands, put one in his right coat pocket and said, "Put your hands on the hand dryer."

Next thing I heard was a thump and Ray's voice: "you can come in now I've got him."

Two agents rushed in and cuffed Grant Jr. Then searched him and took a gun out of his right hand pocket.

Ray then said in his phone, "Have got the parcel and secured, all ok."

One Agent read Grant Jr's arrest out and the next minute two more agents came in and 4 of them took Grant out followed by Ray and me.

Sue came to us and we all left the café. got in our cars and went to the MI5 building.

On arrival at the building, Grant was taken away and Ray, Sue and I, went to Mikes office.
Mike said to us all, "well done but somehow it's been too easy and I'm expecting something or someone to contact and stop us trying to get answers from him. I'm afraid, until then, we go through the usual process of interrogation - trying to tease out any info we can, as we have no solid proof of him actually killing anyone. We have only, threatening with a gun and no doubt he will contact a top-class solicitor when he is allowed to."

Not too far away in a large but secluded house was a cigar smoking Popov; the Russians top man on espionage and organising it.

Opposite him was a tall well-made man just

informing him of Grants capture by MI5.

Well Popov said, "I do not think they have anything on Grant Jr and we have not used him before in the UK." He blew his smoke away and smiled.

The tall man responded with a grin and he replied, "I agree but, can we do anything to recover him?

"Umm" was the reply.

Eventually Popov said "leave it with me and do nothing until I come back on it."

The agent stood to go and out of the blue Popov said, "Can your contact find out if and when they move him to a prison?"

The agent parted saying, "will do" and left.

The following morning, I arrived at MI5 about 9 am and went to Mikes office, knocked the door and a voice said come in. It was Roy and he brought me up to date. Apparently, they had done everything they could to get information out of him to no effect and very soon must let Grant contact a lawyer. When this is done, he will be sent to a prison for safe keeping.

I murmured to Roy, "giving others a chance to contact him?"

Roy nodded a yes, grimacing.

Mike came in and informed us they will take him to a prison later today with full escort and I would like you two to tag along in your car as extra security.

We both nodded yes.

Mike said be ready to go at 1pm, good luck, I've got a feeling we will need it?

Popov, put down his phone having given instructions to do a rescue on MI5's prisoner.

Now they know the route they will take they could get every thing in place they need.

Umm I guess I may be get a call from 'T' soon?

CHAPTER 11

The expected happened.

The convoy of a leading Police car, the prison van and a support car of agents following, set off. Ray and I following at a distance. The prison van followed the police who had decided on the route.

Ray driving the support car said, "I think you will find the police go the long way round to the prison."

I smiled and said I guess they know best, but I think Grants employers will try to release him." I just sat back watching the convoy through his binoculars.

Slowly they did about half the journey, when I said to Ray, "Keep your wits about you, as I know this area and I would try the small wood area down about a mile, and this is next to a field they hold cattle in and its usually a very quiet road."

Ray smiled and slowed down a little so we could manoeuvre either way if they got any signs of an escape attempt.

The police car passed a gate and as the van was not too near following them, it gave Grants rescuers a chance to get a large number of cows inbetween the car and the van.

The police car stopped to turn around, as they did two armed masked men with rifles pointing at them said, "Keep still and quiet, you will not be harmed, but a wrong move - you will not see tomorrow." Both police put their hands on the dashboard as they were told to.

The van drivers assistant had jumped out the van to move the cattle and the man dressed as a farmer just pointed a pistol into his midriff and said, "Just do as your told and you will live, now move to your door and tell your mate to do the same." Which he did walking with the farmer back to his door in the van.
The farmer behind the guard said very firmly, "Now open the van doors and release your prisoner or all will die."

He did what he was told, and the farmer had the prison drivers get in the back and locked it.

Grant ran up the road to a waiting car and climbed in.

Meanwhile, both Ray and I got worried about the length of time they were stopped so walked along the side of the road near the wood ready to use the wood as protection if needed.

We got near the agent's car and then realised the men were all knocked out in the car. We then checked the van and found Grant gone and the two men locked inside it.

Ray got on his phone to HQ and told them.

I had got the men out of the van when Ray got back and told the men to get on their radio.

Grant scrambled in the car waiting for the men who had freed him, and he had been given a raincoat to wear, which he put on before getting in the car with two of the men who had performed the escape.

It took off, the driver turned on to a main road and picked up speed.

After a quarter of an hour Grant asked their

destination and one at front said, "We are taking you to a small cottage near a private airport as we figure you would want to get back to the USA as fast as you could."

Grant smiled and said, "Yes that's what they would think also, so just drop me off and disappear." The driver just nodded a yes and stopped the car near the cottage, then shot off.

Grant found the key and went in. And had a smoke of his favourite cigars.

Back at the place where the prison van had been stopped Ray and I stood waiting for help to appear.

It soon arrived and the cattle were soon back in the field and the empty cleared, prison van drove away with MI5 Agents with more help, set off to try and find a lead on Grants whereabouts.

Mike had joined Ray and I and I had said, "I think there is a small private airport not too far away, I suggest we check there for a start."

Mike nodded yes and gave the order to us to investigate if Grant was there or had been there. Little did they realise Grant still had a contract to fulfill and was on the way to London with this in mind.

Ray and I left the others and drove to the local airport big enough to do private flights to the USA.

Ray used his credentials to talk and make enquiries about Grant and became certain he was not in any way getting a flight here.

We both went to the canteen and talked over the possibilities Grant could take, knowing land, sea and air would by now be covered by MI5.

I said to Ray, "I think we have to give him a bait to go for to get him to make a move when we can be there in numbers and ready. I know I'm the bait. My suggestion, as I've an invite to a new show tomorrow evening in the east end, is it could be a good place to get him to make a move."

Ray looked at me very seriously, stating, "it's a hell of a risk Bret are you sure you want to be put in harms way?"

Smiling I replied, "Well I've done this with you a few times in the forces and it meant depending on each person in the squad including you and it worked."

"Ok" he murmured and rang Mike making my suggestion.

"You Roy do not let Bret out of your or other agent's sight at any time. Just force him to show his hand which we will jump on immediately. Here is what I think we should do."

He finished the call, looked at me and with a rye smile, said, "He instructed us to return to base and he will have a plan ready."

CHAPTER 12

A risk worth taking?

Grant had called his contacts, and it had come back, Bret is invited to attend a new show the next evening and he was attending.

Grant decided to go shopping and pick up items for his disguise. He also decided he would get a chance to get in the theatre to reconnoitre it.

He knew the place to get his disguise, so had soon sorted this for the stage as a fault had been reported.

He then drove to the theatre and having a boiler suit in his boot, took his tool bag and went to the backstage entrance and said, "he had come to check the electricity meters as requested by the management."
He was told to go in.

This gave him a chance to see every room and

the backstage set up. He was shouted back to the entrance and the old man said, "Hi guv, I've just mashed would you like one?"

Grant smiled and replied, "no thanks pop, I have not long had one, but thanks for asking" and carried on into the theatre.

He knew what disguise he was going as, so now to make sure all the necessary things were done before tomorrow, and arrange all he needed to-attend the theatre.

Ray, Sue, and I went over everything a few times and we were happy we had covered everything.

The night came. Bret with Sue went to the reception in a hotel near to the theatre and Roy and several agents were about.

All the guests who would be in our box were introduced including a tall overweight man with plenty of weight and a moustache and beard also, was very loud and obnoxious.
He had a Southern drawl, and on his check-up, MI5 had a good file on him. He also smoked cigars all the while. He also had not brought a partner?

We all left at the same time. I had Ray driving

who commented on the way, they had not spotted Grant but they are ready if he does appear.

We got in the box and sat at our seats and I noted the American banker sat the nearest to the door, so we were all ready to see this new British musical show.

Ray had stationed agents in specific places he had decided on and he had put himself on the high walkway behind the stage which gave him a good view of the box Sue and I sat in.

He figured with his snipers rifle anyone in the box was covered in a second of needing any assistance.

The show began with a song they all had heard many times now on television and radio and supported by dancers. After 45 minutes there was an interval and most in the box left to get some refreshment including Sue who said to me, "I wont be long, don't worry Ray is keeping his eye on you from above, I wont be long" and she left.

The big American remained with just myself. He politely said to me, "Nice girl that! You will have to marry her" his mistake! No one in this company knew I was not married, and they all took her as his wife.

I smiled and said, "thanks but I thought you would have gone for a smoke of your cigars?" I was feeling at the same time for my phone in my pocket which I felt and pressed the phone button no one could hear, for agent in trouble.

The American said "I thought we could both go together?"

I replied, "sorry I will wait here for Sue."

He looked at me and said, "I want you to and if you look at my right hand in the pocket I have a gun aimed at you so please lets go".
I put my hands up a little to indicate he was pointing a gun at me and he said. "Put your hands down."

I did. Then I heard a phut sound and Grant stood for a few seconds with a hole in his forehead, then fell backwards . At the same time Sue and two agents came in with guns in their hand and one said, "he's dead alright."

I sat down while the agents sorted Grant's body out, "are you ok?"

I looked at Sue, smiled and replied, "Yes ok just

cannot get over the fact I could swear I heard the bullet go by and felt the draft as it did." Shaking my head.

She smiled, then grimaced saying, "That's Ray for you and it's a good job he is a crack shot!"

"Too right" I murmured.

Sue then had a phone call and after she answered it turned and said, "We are wanted back at MI5." So we set off and had two agents who Sue knew, go with us.
Ray was waiting for us, and he took us to Mike's office.

They were debriefed and when it was finished Mike asked me, if I needed a rest and being very interested in the sudden change in Mikes voice I said, "Let's get it all done now - that needs doing."

Mike smiled and said, "I have been informed just an hour ago they have found your friend Arthur alive, and he will be arriving in England tomorrow. I have set a meeting up with all of us tomorrow to meet and greet. I also know the position it puts you in Bret, but no doubt you will sort that out."

I said, "That's great news and I look forward to it

as I never wanted to be wealthy to the extent I now am and I will be glad to see him again."

Mike smiling said, "I've ordered a whisky to be brought in and let's drink to getting Grant." Then, looking at me, "To all your safe keeping and here's giving the Russians a thick ear."

We all raised our glasses.
I went to my hotel and sat a while thinking on the past few hours and eventually it came back to me about the appearance of Arthur and how he had been found alive.

I picked up my phone, rang my solicitor and explained about the reappearance of Arthur and the shares and transferred money I felt I should return.

His reply was, "Thanks for the information, but I will have to look up what is the system of returning the inheritance and will come back on it."

I had a shower and early to bed.

CHAPTER 13

A strange reunion.

I set out to meet Mike and Sue at the place they were keeping Arthur and we all went in the same car driven by Ray. We all went together and rang the front door bell.

We were put in a room that was a pleasantly furnished lounge with two settees and numerous easy chairs near small coffee tables and we were provided with tea or coffee.

The person who was a butler and main help for anything else we required, brought the teas and coffees, plus answered any questions we enquired about Arthur he could answer.

When Arthur arrived with a MI5 doctor and nurse with him, he sat near us on an easy chair talking and laughing.

When I got my turn, I started to talk about the

times in the forces and some of the escapades Arthur and I did, plus one or two when we had Mike and Ray with us. But none of them could he remember, even when I prompted him on the ones we did together, he could not offer anything on them. Strange!! He did however show more memory of recent occurrences and events.

After I saw Arthur again, and not having other people about, I did manage a short conversation with him, but I still had a niggle in myself, that he was not really who he says he is.

Later in the morning I mentioned to Ray did he know when Arthur's PA was coming to see him.

He replied, "As a matter of fact she will be here at 2 o'clock today".

I said, "Then I shall be here to watch it," as I knew the room they would be using had a one-way glass window in it.
So, Ray and I and later Sue, joined us for a quick sandwich and drink, in a small pub not far away from where Arthur was staying.

We arrived back and the three of us settled ourselves in the room with the one-way glass in. We sat talking and debating a football match this weekend. When it was announced the PA had arrived, Sue left as she was escorting the PA.

We watched the PA come in and say to Arthur, "I'm very glad to see you again," hugged him and stood back with tears in her eyes! He did not show a lot of affection and she looked very upset as he did not!

He then started to speak to the agent near him saying he was tired and would like somewhere to rest. The agent took him out of the room.

I said to Ray, "I thought she was very close when I last met him, mmm?"

Ray picked up the phone and spoke to Mike. Turned to me and said, "They have several recordings of Arthur speaking at functions and none match his voice now, so they are planning to let him into the world he was in but, we will be either there or close at hand, would I help out?"

I nodded a yes.

"Bret we would like you to get to know him and get as friendly as it is safe to do so!" said Ray.

I smiled and nodded yes.

So as the days went by, I met him and we went one or two places to find out more about his intended life.

Although he never invited his PA to go anywhere with him. I still had Sue's company and always had her join me.

He eventually asked us to go to see the land in Norfolk next to the land the Russian's had.

CHAPTER 14

The last chance.

Sue and I, with Arthur set off to look at the area around the land still to develop. We could not see anything of the land now taken over by the government from the Russians. There was a lot of helicopters. The MOD was about and had engines revving on the land now taken over by them.

The land I was to develop was as I had last seen it and the only difference were more MOD notices on the fences.

I did comment that it was pointless developing the older people's bungalows idea, due to the noise.

Arthur never said anything, just looked.
Having seen it and Arthur's silence, I suggested we go to a small public house down the road and get a snack before we explore the area more.

When we settled into our seats, Arthur said "to

excuse him" and went towards the men's room.

Sue and I chose our snack and he had said he would have the same. We went back to the table.

It wasn't long before Arthur returned, and when I turned to tell him we had ordered a BLT and gin and tonic, he nodded okay. As I turned back I felt I was being watched by a male on his own at a nearby table who seemed to have an interest in us. That's interesting I thought. I looked again and he was going.

I arrived at the Hotel with Sue as my escort, I suggested a walk along the cliff path from the hotel.

She said, "I will change and catch you up as I have a couple of phone calls to make, I'm sure you can look after yourself for a short walk? Just keep your eyes open and take care, you have your phone." smiled and went to the lift.
I went along the garden path to the cliff path and slowly walked along it to the fence that adjoined the property I'm supposed to own now. I went to a spot, that was well hidden, but I could see everything I wanted too and quietly sat on a tree stump looking through my binoculars.

Sue had finished her calls, changed and set out in slacks and a dark coloured coat.

I had by chance heard two people talking not too far away but I could not see them, so I silently moved trough the bushes to the spot I thought the conversation was coming from.

I went to go through a bush and stopped. Then moved more to my left and slowly parted the shrubs and realised I had come across Arthur and another man who looked like the one in the pub, deep in conversation in what to me sounded like Russian.

I recorded some on my phone and was about to go back the way I had come when a female hand stopped me very softly saying, "Hold on Bret I want a listen, they are speaking Russian."

Sue also was recording it on her phone.

They stayed about ten minutes and they stopped and left separately in different directions.

Sue then said when they were far enough away, "They were both planning to dispose of someone and my guess it is you, Bret!"

I gave a smile and replied, "We better get prepared then, hadn't we" I put my arm on her shoulder and gave it a squeeze and we set off back to the hotel.

Back at the hotel we went to Sue's room, and she contacted Mike at MI5. I made a cup of tea, and she joined me. Sue sat in the chair and I sat on the bed and she brought me up to date on her new instructions.

She said, "Mike has sent Ray by helicopter so he should be here tonight. There are other agents arriving as well. Mike now knows Arthur is a fake, a Russian plant, and we also want everyone connected with him."

"As far as you are concerned, I have got to be with you 24 hours a day, so back to our routine."

I smiled and said, "I will do that and I intend to be in at the finish, its my mate he is impersonating."

She looked at me and said, "I thought you would!"

So that evening we had dinner with Arthur knowing all we did know.

He left early and Sue and I had a nightcap of a gin and tonic and during our conversation I accidently let out what my doctor had told me the day before I left. He said, I had cancer of the prostate, and will be on treatment after a few more tests. I asked her to keep it to herself. She had nodded yes.

Sue's phone rang and she answered with a couple of yes's and turned to me saying, "That was Ray and Arthur is in the same place he went too yesterday waiting for his contact."

We had already made sure we had dark clothes on and set off down the path.
As we approached the area we got to yesterday, we could hear voices in Russian and very slowly made our way until we could see them. It was the same man he met yesterday but both had dark clothes on and Sue picked up they were planning to get rid of me tonight.

I quietly said to Sue "I will take Arthur. You take the other man and with guns in hand we burst through the shrubs saying, "MI5, get your hands up high where we can see them, your games well and truly up."

They both froze facing us and slowly raised their hands and looked at me with the most evil looks I've ever seen.

Sue said, "Now face the fence and straddle your legs and hands on the fence", which they both did. She went up to them, kicked their legs further apart and took the other man's gun and threw it away on the grass.

The other man looked at her doing the same to Arthur and as she reached for Arthur's gun, he hit her hard in the face, dropped down to one knee and with a knife he had in his sleeve, threw it at me. I felt a pain in my chest, but as I slowly went down fired a couple of rounds.

Next second another gun fired two rounds that hit Arthur and the other man Ray, who was quickly joined by two agents, looked at Bret and Sue who were being cared for by the other agents who had appeared.

Bret was dead! Sues face was cut but not hurt otherwise.

Sue will always remember this day in Norfolk and on the ground, a dead Bret.

Very soon there were four stretchers with medics looking at Bret and Sue. The two men were taken away and Sue and Ray both went with Bret in an ambulance.

One year later on the same date, a group of people met up in the Norfolk hotel. A meal had been put on and all were talking to one another.

They all filled their glasses for a toast to be given by Ray, "To a friend and colleague who gave his life for his country and someone we will always remember on this date by all here, for ever!

Lift your glass to BRET MANN" Sue wiped her eyes, she had kept her word, she had told no one he had cancer!

One or two of the ladies held handkerchiefs to their eyes as well but no one else knew what Bret had told Sue before he was killed...

Printed in Great Britain
by Amazon